PIMPLE'S
CHRISTMAS

or...
'That's what makes you special'

Gilly Goodwin

Cover designed by Cover Creator and Mastersound Studios
Pictures supplied by Shutterstock, 123RF and Mastersound Studios.

First Printing: Dec 2019

ISBN: 978-1-7128-5823-3

CHAPTER ONE

Pimple is lonely

The forest lay blanketed in snow and a tiny robin fluttered towards the tallest tree and landed on a wintry branch.

On the alert for any movement, the robin noticed a small deer stepping carefully in the snow.

Thick snowflakes fell on the deer's eyelashes and nose, making him sneeze.

'Hello,' the robin tweeted gently, not wanting to startle him. 'Where is your herd?'

The deer sniffed and one tear rolled down his soft, furry cheek.

'I don't know – I'm lost. The snow has covered their tracks.' He looked up at the robin. 'I'm lonely; will you be my friend?'

'I'm lonely too; my family have flown away for the winter,' the little robin blinked rapidly.

'Whoo-hoo-hoo,' a wise old owl perching on a nearby branch, hooted loudly, making them jump in fright.

'Whoo-hoo-hoo! Why don't you find *the lonely elf?* He says he has a clever plan.'

'Oh thank you Professor Owl' said the robin.

The little robin looked hopefully at the deer ... 'will you come with me to look for him?'

'Yes please,' the deer nodded.

The robin proudly puffed up his chest; 'my name is Rusty, what is your name?'

'Pimple,' the deer said shyly.

Rusty smiled. 'What kind of name is that?'

'If you travel on my head you will understand.'

Rusty flew onto the deer's head and noticed two small pink pimples where the antlers had just started to grow.

'Ouch, they look sore,' twittered Rusty.

'They're itchy,' Pimple bleated. 'I keep scratching my head against the trees.'

There was an answering bleat from behind a nearby tree.

'Who's that?' Pimple called out.

A small white lamb with a black spot on the top of each ear appeared from around the tree.

The robin proudly puffed up his chest, 'my name is Rusty; this is Pimple. What is your name?'

'I'm Little Lambert,' bleated the lamb. 'I'm lost and lonely – I can't find my flock in the snow.' Little Lambert looked all around him. 'The snow is too thick and too fluffy.'

'We are lonely too. We have been told that *the lonely elf* will help us ... will you come with us?' Pimple said to Little Lambert.

'Oh yes please,' Little Lambert's tail waggled slightly.

CHAPTER TWO

The search for the lonely elf

The new friends started their journey, but it was a long way and as the light faded, the moon peeped through the clouds and one star began to twinkle.

Rusty flew high into the air and called up to the star ... 'we are lonely and lost. Can you help us?'

'I am lonely too,' said the star, and she started to fade a little.

Pimple looked up; 'hello, my name is Pimple, this is Rusty and here is Little Lambert. What is your name?'

'I'm Stella,' said the star. 'My sister-stars are hidden by snow clouds and I can't find them; the clouds are too thick and too fluffy.' She twinkled a little and then started to fade as a small cloud passed in front of her.

'We are going to find *the lonely elf.* He has a clever plan. Will you come with us?' Pimple said to Stella.

'Oh yes please,' Stella started to twinkle. 'I saw *the lonely elf* a few days ago. He said he was searching for Santa Claus to find work for Christmas.'

Stella floated across the sky, shining all around. Pimple set off to follow the star with Rusty perched on his head and Little Lambert following sheepishly behind!

Stella drifted a few miles, until she stopped over a small wooden hut.

A young elf appeared in the doorway looking a bit surprised.

Pimple stepped forward. 'Hello, are you *the lonely elf?* We've been told you have a clever plan.'

Gilly Goodwin

CHAPTER THREE

The clever plan

'Hello,' said the elf. 'My name is Elvis. I *was* lonely but I came to work for Santa Claus and he says he will find me a new family in time for Christmas.'

'We would like to find a new family too,' Little Lambert bleated excitedly. Rusty tweeted in agreement and Stella twinkled brightly ... but Pimple was too busy scratching his head on a nearby tree.

Elvis took them to find Santa who listened carefully to their story and smiled at the three friends.

'So Pimple...' he said. 'Why are you lonely and where is your herd?'

'They made fun of my pimples,' Pimple said sadly, showing Santa his itchy, pink lumps. 'They all have strong antlers ... but mine won't grow.'

'You are still young, Pimple; don't be in such a rush to grow up. Your antlers will soon grow strong and tall. They are what will make you special.'

Santa smiled kindly and rubbed the deer's itchy pimples.

'So Rusty...' said Santa. 'What a good name ... and that's a lovely colour.'

'But my chest should be bright red,' tweeted the robin. 'All my friends have red feathers.'

'You are still young, Rusty; don't be in such a rush to grow up. Your feathers will soon glow brightly. They are what will make you special.'

Santa smiled kindly and gently stroked the robin's proud chest.

'Little Lambert … well you are a sweet little lamb. I love the black spots on your ears,' said Santa kindly.

Little Lambert waggled his tail. 'But my flock are all white. No black spots - so I can't find them in the snow … and I'm cold!' added Little Lambert with a shiver.

'You are still young Little Lambert; don't be in such a rush to grow up. Your woollen coat will soon grow and keep you warm. It is what will make you special.'

Santa smiled kindly and gently pulled Little Lambert's ears.

Santa gazed up at the twinkling star. 'Stella, why are you lonely? There are a lot of stars in the dark sky.'

'But they are all hidden behind the clouds, except me ... because I am so bright.' Stella tried to hide behind a cloud.

'You are still young, Stella; don't be in such a rush to grow up. You will soon be the brightest star in the heavens and wise men will choose to follow you. It is what will make you special.'

Santa smiled kindly, shielding his eyes from the dazzling light.

Pimple, Rusty, Little Lambert and Stella all smiled shyly at Santa.

Elvis came forward, shaking each foot in turn, trying to keep the snow out of his dirty, ripped shoes. 'But we are still lonely and you said you would help us find another family in time for Christmas.'

Elvis's voice shook as he shivered in the frosty air.

CHAPTER FOUR

A new home and family

Santa took pity on them all, and led them into his workshop while Stella kept watch above the doorway ... then he made special arrangements for them all to have a new festive family.

Three days later, on Christmas Eve … bright lights shone from the windows of a cosy cottage near the edge of the forest. A large Christmas tree stood in the corner of a room near a log fire.

Traditional ornaments and tinsel were joined by some 'special' new additions.

Stella had pride of place, shining brightly on the top of the tree.

Rusty was perched on a high branch with his feathers glowing in the firelight.

Little Lambert wasn't far away ... dangling happily and wearing a new woollen fleece.

Pimple looked up from his own branch and proudly shook his splendid new antlers.

Elvis grinned as he balanced near the trunk of the tree ... wearing a new pair of soft, blue shoes.

(But that's another story)

Gilly Goodwin

The End

Gilly Goodwin

ABOUT THE AUTHOR

Gilly Goodwin is an author, music teacher and composer. She has written a number of children's stories and a middle-grade novel – **Uriel ... A Whisper of Wings;** the first book of a trilogy intended for readers aged approx. 9-14 ... *and for any adults who have not completely given up their childhood!* See further details below.

As a Composer (using the name Gilly Goldsmith) she has published the first volume of a book of new and original Carols -intended for various choral ensembles from SSA through to SATB.

Count the Angels incorporates various musical styles from traditional – to light pop music.

Count the Angels is available as a paperback and ebook on Amazon and in other bookstores. Look out for Volume two!

The soundtracks are also available on CD from Amazon.

Gilly also composes choral works/ some sacred works/ songs and TV themes. She lives with her husband in Southport (UK) and has two grown-up children. She loves all animals – particularly dogs and has recently owned two springer spaniels – Holly and Jazzy.

Uriel ... A Whisper of Wings

This is a traditional adventure story (with elements of humour and fantasy) where three lively children (and their dog) are granted an inadvertent wish and embark on a strange, perilous adventure in another world. They are shocked by the arrival of Uriel, a fair youth who appears suddenly in their playroom, spouts poetry, and claims ownership of the empty treasure chest they found in the sand dunes. Uriel sends the three siblings on a rescue mission to find the Wilton boys (their bad-tempered bullies) and to recover his birth-right; a fantastic 'treasure' – stolen and guarded by a terrifying, smoky apparition.

But who is Uriel ... and why do they keep hearing the faint whisper of wings?

Uriel ... A Whisper of Wings is intended to be the first part of a trilogy and was particularly influenced by a fascination with the conversations between C.S. Lewis and J.R.R. Tolkien where they discuss the hidden messages in their novels and argue whether those messages should be deeply hidden in the text or made more obvious to the reader.

Uriel ... A Whisper of Wings is available as an ebook and paperback on Amazon and in other bookstores.

Please leave me a review.
Thank you
Gilly Goodwin

Pictures taken from **Uriel ... A Whisper of Wings** and **Count the Angels**

Made in the USA
Middletown, DE
07 November 2022

14310801R00015